This book is dedicated to
Eddie, Edna, George, David,
Patrick, Britt, and United
AirLines
                Love,
                    Todd

Copyright © 1999 by Todd Parr

First Edition

Library of Congress Cataloging-in-Publication Data
Parr, Todd.
   Things that make you feel good/things that make you feel bad /
   Todd Parr. — 1st ed.
      p.   cm.
   Summary: An illustrated list of twelve good things, like bubble baths and
bedtime stories, and twelve things that are not so nice, like chicken pox and
mosquito bites.
   ISBN 0-316-69270-0
   [1. Emotions — Fiction.] I. Title.
PZ7.P2447Tg 1999
[E] — dc21   98-13081

10 9 8 7 6 5 4 3

TWP

Printed in Singapore

THiNGS THAT MAKE YOU FEEL GOOD
THiNGS THAT MAKE YOU FEEL BaD

TODD PARR

Megan Tingley Books

Little, Brown and Company
Boston New York London

Good

Bubble baths

Good

maCaroni
and
Cheese

Tummy aches

Good

Pets

Stink BUGS

Good

Hot chocolate with
marshmallows

Good

Friends

Bad

Bullies

Bad

Toothache

Good

Sun

Bad

The
Dark

Good

kisses

Good

Waves

Bad

Sharks

Good

Book Book Book

Book Book Book

Bedtime Stories

chicken soup

chicken pox

BiG birthday presents

Bad

BiG Hairy spiders